ALISON SAVES THE WEDDING
by Catherine Connor

Illustrations by
Gabriel Picart

Spot Illustrations by
Rich Grote

MAGIC ATTIC PRESS

As members of the
MAGIC ATTIC CLUB,
we promise to
be best friends,
share all of our adventures in the attic,
use our imaginations,
have lots of fun together,
and remember—the real magic is in us.

Alison   Keisha

Heather   Megan

Contents

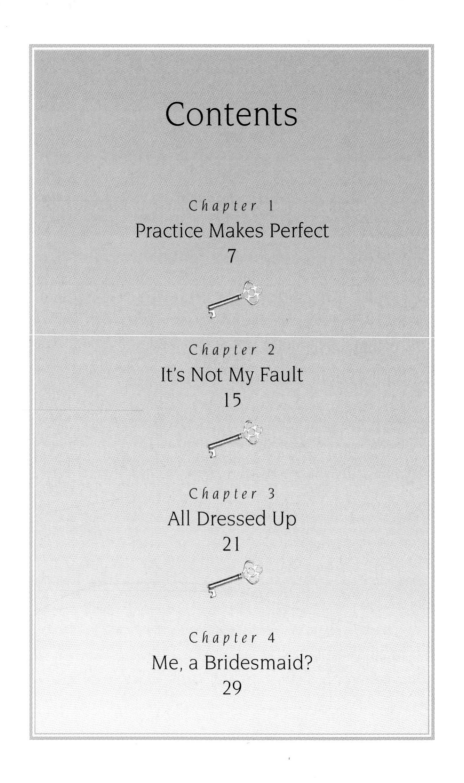

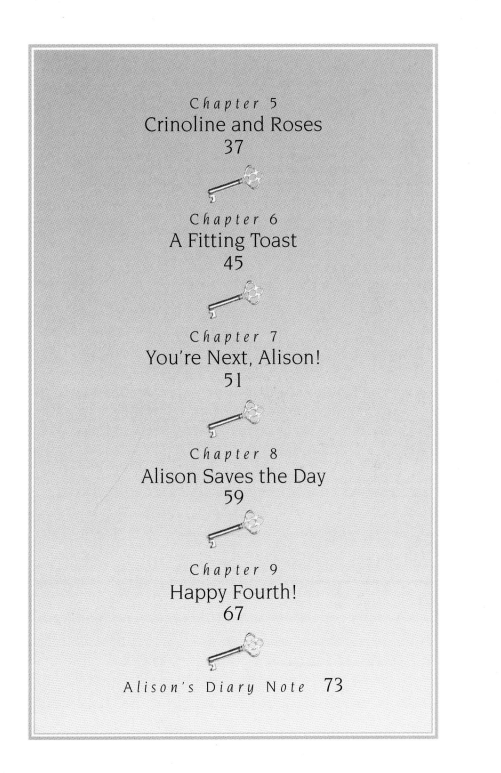

Chapter One

PRACTICE MAKES PERFECT

 kay, everybody," shouted Alison McCann, "we have to do something more spectacular! How about some wheelies!"

"Great!" said Keisha Vance, but Megan Ryder and Heather Hardin brought their bikes to a dead stop in the middle of the parking lot.

"Ali," said Heather, "we aren't going to look very good in the Fourth of July parade if we're all in bandages and casts."

Alison laughed. "All right, Keisha and I can do wheelies,

and you and Megan invent something safer that won't ruin your ballet career."

Heather breathed a sigh of relief. The four best friends had been rehearsing all morning. Alison had talked them into entering the parade as a "precision bike-riding team." They all loved to ride their bikes, and they found the empty paved lot a perfect place to rehearse.

Alison, the best athelete of the four and absolutely fearless on her bicycle, was the "choreographer" for the team. She was really challenging her friends, dreaming up more and more difficult moves to dazzle the parade judges.

"We have to win a trophy!" Alison urged the three girls.

"I just want to be in the parade for the fun of it," said Megan.

"Me, too," said Keisha. "It doesn't really matter if we win or not."

"I can't believe what I'm hearing," said Alison. "What's the point of entering if we don't want to win?"

"Oh, Ali," said Heather, "I think you want to win just because Mark got a second-place trophy in last year's parade."

"Admit it," Megan said with a laugh. "You live to

compete with your brother Mark because he can beat you in so many sports."

They're right, thought Alison. I'd love to see the look on Mark's face if I brought home a first-place trophy. "Hey, let's take a break and decide on our costumes," she suggested, eager to change the subject.

Keisha nodded. "Heather, you're the artist. Got any good ideas?"

The four girls giggled as Heather, her cheeks flushing, curtsied and told them her ideas. They could decorate their bicycle helmets with ribbons and flowers, and Heather's mom would help them paint designs on bright, solid-color T shirts and shorts.

"This is going to be so cool!" Keisha exclaimed.

"We should wear socks that match our shirts and paint designs on our sneakers, too," suggested Alison.

"Great idea!" said Megan.

Keisha frowned. "I don't know if my mother will let me paint my sneakers."

"Keish, it's not like they're just going to be splattered with paint," said Alison. "Heather's mom is an artist. They'll probably be more valuable after they're painted."

"Real works of art," Megan added.

Alison's eyes glowed. "Hey, we might even win a Best Costume award!"

"Ali," said Keisha, cocking her head, "we're doing this for fun, remember?"

"You're right," Alison replied, "but competing is fun, too. Our bike routine will knock those judges' socks off."

"We have so many moves, I can hardly remember them all," Keisha continued. "Let's see, there's the precision turn, the figure eight, the big circle—"

"And I have this great idea for a slalom course—"

"Yikes!" Heather interrupted Alison. "Let's stop before she sends us all to the hospital!"

"Right," said Keisha, laughing. "It's lunchtime anyway."

"Oh, okay," Alison replied with exaggerated reluctance. She didn't mind stopping; she was getting pretty hungry. "But let's meet at my house at three," she added with a grin, "so we can practice some more."

The girls nodded and pedaled away, waving to Alison as she sped on ahead. Alison practiced her slalom moves as she wheeled into her driveway.

Her twin brothers were in the front yard, tossing a softball. Showing off a bit, Steven threw the ball hard, and it hit Jason in the forehead. He fell to the ground with a howl.

Alison sprang off her bike and ran to see if he was all right. Jason stood bravely while she looked at his head. She gave him a hug and wiped a tear off his cheek. "Hey, big guy, you'd better remember to wear your batting helmet, or we'll have to trade this noggin in for a Mr. Potato Head!" she said. The boys were laughing as they all went inside.

The kitchen was in its usual state of creative chaos with Mrs. McCann's catering business and the family's meals competing for space. Mrs. McCann sent the boys to wash up and asked Alison to help her carry lunch into the dining room. Alison smiled when she saw that her father was home. The house he was going to show to prospective buyers that afternoon was nearby, so he had decided to come home to have lunch with the family.

"Dad, you should see all the neat moves I came up with for our precision bike team," said Alison.

"That's great, honey," Mr. McCann replied.

"You guys will probably crash in a big pile of spokes, and we'll have to get the Jaws of Life to untangle you," teased Mark.

This time, the teasing didn't bother Alison, and she made a funny face at him. "You're just envious that you're not on the team," she said. But it was hard not to think of the whole Magic Attic Club in a pileup in the middle of the parade. That's not going to happen, Alison promised herself. We're going to be great!

After lunch, as Alison was rinsing the dishes and placing them in the dishwasher, she heard her father's car backing down the driveway. Suddenly there was a horrible scraping sound.

"What was that?" asked her mother.

"Oh, no!" shouted Alison, racing for the door.

Chapter

Two

IT'S NOT MY FAULT

lison ran across the lawn, screaming, "Dad! Dad!"

Mr. McCann stopped the car and got out. "What was *that*?" he asked, looking worriedly at Alison.

"Dad, my bike's hooked on your bumper!" Alison pointed to the rear of the car.

"Alison!" He shouted angrily. "You left it in the driveway, didn't you?" Alison could only stare at the crumpled bike and try to fight back the tears. "How many times have I told you not to leave things lying around?" Her father yanked the bike free of the bumper.

"About a million," said Alison. "But I was trying to help Jason—"

"I don't want to hear any excuses. This is your own fault, Alison."

Alison knew he was right, and she was furious with herself. She had forgotten all about her bike, and now it was ruined.

"Take this mess away," her father said, as he handed the bike over to her. "I'm running late. We'll discuss it when I get home." With that, he got back into his car and drove away.

Sniffling, Alison slowly dragged the bike into the garage, dumped it on the floor, and after giving it a kick for good measure, dejectedly plopped down beside it.

"Mom, what am I going to do?" Alison cried out when Mrs. McCann and the boys came out to see what had happened. "I *have* to have a bike!"

"You do have one, Alison, though it's not much to look at anymore," her mother replied.

"Anybody can have an accident!" Alison wailed.

Her mother gave her a long look, then said quietly, "When your father gets home, you can ask him to help you fix it." She turned to the door. "Come on, boys, leave your sister alone now. You have chores to do."

Later in the afternoon, Alison was waiting in the garage when her father returned. She promised him she would never leave anything in the driveway again, and he agreed to try to repair the bike if she would help. Mark came out to lend a hand.

It didn't take that long to get the wheels turning and the handlebars aligned, but the fenders were badly dented, and big sections of paint had been scraped away.

"Well, it runs," said Mark, "and I think you're going to win a special prize—for the *ugliest* bike in the parade."

Alison was glaring at her brother, trying to think of a retort, as Keisha, Heather, and Megan rode up. When they wheeled into the open garage, Heather let out a shriek.

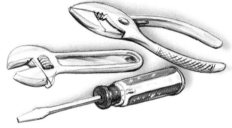

"Omigosh, Ali," said Megan. "Is that your bike?"

"You mean *was* that her bike," said Keisha.

"Dad's car mangled it," Alison responded sadly.

"Boy, you're not kidding," said Heather. "It looks like it went through the garbage disposal."

"What are you going to ride in the parade?" asked Megan.

"I don't know," Alison replied. "I can't ride this mess."

"Well, it's good enough for practice," said Keisha. "Let's go."

"I'm sorry," said Alison. "I'm just not in the mood to practice anymore today. Maybe I won't even be in the parade. You three can have your own team."

"Oh, Ali, we don't want to do that," Heather protested.

"We're all a team," said Keisha.

"You have to ride," pleaded Megan. "You're the captain."

Alison turned to her father. "I have to have a new bike," she said.

"This bicycle is less than a year old, Alison," Mr McCann answered as he put away his tools.

"But, Dad," Alison protested, "what am I supposed to ride in the parade?"

"You can't have everything you want, Alison. Especially not until you prove you can take care of your belongings."

"Well, I didn't do it on purpose!" Alison snapped back.

Before Mr. McCann could reply, Heather cut in. "I think we'd better go, Ali."

"Riiight," said Keisha, "I . . . uh . . . have to baby-sit."

"Bye," said Megan, sounding relieved. "I'll call you later."

The three girls wheeled down the driveway.

Alison leaned her battered bike against the wall, gave it a disgusted look, and followed her father into the kitchen. Maybe a different approach would be better.

"Dad, you wouldn't drive around in a wrecked car, would you?" Alison asked. "So why should I have to ride around on a wrecked bike?"

"Forget it, Ali," her father said. "If you want to start saving your money, we'll match your savings and help you buy a new one."

"But, Dad, that could take months. Maybe years. I need a new bike by the Fourth of July."

"Alison, the answer is no," said her mother. "Sometimes you just have to make the best of a bad situation."

"Oh, great," said Alison. "That means I can't ride in the parade."

"Why not?" asked Mr. McCann. "It runs fine."

"I'd be the laughingstock of the day—of the whole summer."

"Alison!" said her father. "I'm surprised at you. You're no quitter."

Chapter Three

ALL DRESSED UP

 t's not fair, thought Alison. I was doing a good deed helping Jason, and look what I got for it. I can just picture myself riding that banged-up bike in front of the parade judges while the whole crowd laughs at me.

She grabbed her pillow and smacked it against the quilt, then flopped onto her bed and stared at the ceiling.

Usually she loved being in her bedroom, but today it offered no comfort.

"Nuts!" Alison said aloud, raising her head. She bounced off the bed, ran out of the house, and headed next door to Ellie Goodwin's white Victorian house. She raced up the steps and rang the bell. Ever since she and Heather, Keisha, and Megan had discovered the endless supply of outfits in Ellie's attic and had their first amazing adventure by looking in her mirror, the attic had been one of Alison's favorite places to go.

Ellie greeted her warmly and invited her into the sitting room. Today her long hair hung in a silvery braid down her back. "I'm awaiting my next student," she said, "a talented young soprano. I think she could have a career in the opera someday."

"That's great," Alison said politely. Then she launched into a dramatic retelling of her afternoon, complete with sound effects of the bike being dragged down the driveway. She was still kicking herself for having been so forgetful about her bike, especially since the bike-riding team had been her idea.

"What a dilemma," said Ellie. "Surely you don't want to give up being in the parade, do you?"

Alison shook her head.

"You know," Ellie said, "I've learned so much in my

travels over the years. For instance, in Chinese the same character means both 'crisis' and 'opportunity.'" She smiled at Alison as though this revelation would help her.

Alison stared at her. She didn't want to let on that she had no idea what Ellie was talking about, but her expression must have given her away.

"A lot of people have trouble understanding that idea, Alison," Ellie said, rising when the doorbell rang. "Some say it means that when you have the one, you always have the other as well. Think about it for awhile." Ellie smiled, then went to greet her pupil.

Alison leaned her elbows on her knees and stared at the carved feet of the sofa for a few minutes. She couldn't help thinking of the first trip she and Heather, Megan, and Keisha had taken through the mirror and how they had formed the Magic Attic Club when they returned. It was definitely time to go to the attic. Alison plucked the key from its silver box in the entryway and took the stairs two at a time, hoping that whatever adventure awaited her today, it would take her mind off her bike.

The old steamer trunk in Ellie's attic always seemed

to be filled with new outfits, and Alison went straight to it. As she sorted through the clothes, her favorite color caught her eye. She carefully lifted the fabric from under the layers of other clothes. It turned out to be a long, ruffled, pale blue dress with tiny white hearts sprinkled all over it. A pink satin sash at the waist was tied in a bow and topped off with a pink silk flower.

This is definitely not for me, thought Alison. I'll look for something else. She went to the big mahogany wardrobe against the wall. As she poked through its contents, a pair of white shoes tumbled off a shelf. They had pink flowers on them, matching the waistline of the dress. A small pile of flowers in the same soft pink turned out to be a delicate coronet. Alison held the circlet of silk petals in her palm for a minute.

"Pretty," she said aloud, "but not my style." When she set the shoes and crown to one side and walked around the room, she saw all sorts of things that she hadn't noticed before. A small drawer in the desk was open, revealing dozens of packets of tiny glass beads and embroidered ribbon. A set of gold-rimmed cups and saucers, hardly any bigger than a doll's tea set, was stacked on

a shelf beside six ornately cut crystal goblets. On another shelf she found a collection of beautiful dolls in folk costumes.

Alison put aside one piece of clothing after another, still searching for something that might promise a fun adventure. Her attention kept coming back to the blue dress. It must be for some fancy party or something, she thought. If I wear that, I'll probably end up having to sit around and act ladylike and be bored to tears.

It was hardly an outfit for playing basketball or hiking in the woods, Alison thought. Mark sometimes called her his biggest little brother. He said she would probably wear a sweatsuit to her senior prom. Alison knew he was joking, but even the memory of it was upsetting.

"I could do the fashion thing if I wanted to," she said out loud. She stared at the long blue dress beside the trunk. "I could wear this and still look totally cool." She hurriedly stepped out of her bike-riding clothes and into the dress and shoes. They fit perfectly, and she felt very grown-up.

As she adjusted the flower coronet on her blond hair, Alison turned to the tall, gold-framed mirror and looked at herself in amazement. She twirled around, admiring her new look. As she spun, she heard classical music. Could it be coming from the student downstairs? It

sounded live, not like a radio or television concert.

Suddenly the music became clearer, and Alison found herself on the second-floor balcony of a beautiful, rambling old white house, looking down into a garden where a string quartet was warming up. Rows of chairs faced an archway of flowering vines, and big bouquets of white roses tied with white satin ribbons decorated the end of each row.

"It must be a wedding," she whispered to herself. "But whose? And where?"

"You must be Alison," said a voice behind her.

Alison jumped. Three young women were approaching—dressed in blue dresses just like hers!

"Jenny wants us to come to her room," one of the girls called to Alison.

"She wants help getting ready," said another, "and that's part of our responsibility as bridesmaids."

One of the young women grabbed Alison's hand and led her down the long hallway. A molasses-colored cocker spaniel barked at them as they sped up the stairs.

Chapter
Four

ME, A BRIDESMAID?

he young women introduced themselves as Whitney, Kelly, and Danielle as they hurried Alison into a room off another hallway. She came face to face with a young blond woman in a long robe with a puffy crinoline petticoat peeking out. Behind her, a bridal gown and veil hung over the closet doors. This must be Jenny, the bride, thought Alison. I wonder who she thinks I am.

They stared at each other for a long moment. "Alison?" said Jenny. "I haven't seen you since you were a baby!"

A nervous-looking woman came up and planted a quick kiss on Alison's cheek. "You look lovely, my dear, very grown up." Then she turned to run her finger down a long, narrow checklist, mumbling. "Punch, soda, juice. Check tables, get someone to count chairs—"

"Mother! Would you please let the caterer take care of all that? I need you to help me get ready. The ceremony's in less than an hour."

"Oh, Jennifer, you're right, of course." The woman stuffed the list into her pocket. "Now, where's your curling iron? It has to be plugged in for five minutes before we can do your hair." She looked around distractedly and finally focused on Alison. "Alison, could you find it for me? It must be here somewhere."

At that moment the cocker spaniel dashed in, leaped into Jenny's lap, and began licking her cheek. Its stubby tail whipped back and forth, wiggling the dog's whole back end with it.

"Norton! Get out of here!" Jenny's mother screamed, and the dog shot out of the room.

"Mrs. Morris, come quick!" shouted a girl from the bedroom doorway. "The caterer says there's something wrong with the cake!" Jenny's mother raced out the door.

"Oh, no!" cried Jenny. "I can't deal with this. Come on, girls."

"Jenny, you're only half-dressed!" shouted Whitney.

"I don't care," said Jenny, practically in tears. "I have to see." She dashed away, still dressed in her robe. The three older bridesmaids glanced at one another, then hurried after the bride-to-be.

Alison hesitated. Probably there was nothing she could do to help downstairs anyhow. She leaned over and picked up the curling iron and set it on the dressing table. It seemed strangely quiet after all the excitement of a few minutes before. Alison reached out to feel the glossy satin and delicate lace of Jenny's wedding gown. From its perch on the closet door, the veil billowed out as a breeze from the open window caught it.

I wonder what it feels like to be in Jenny's shoes, as Mom would say, Alison asked herself, reaching out and carefully pulling the veil off the door. Stepping over to Jenny's mirror, she set the veil over the coronet of pink petals on her own blond hair, which was much longer than Jenny's. "Kind of weird," she said out loud, "but not bad, I guess."

"No, it's not bad—if you're Jenny," said a voice.

Alison jumped in alarm. A boy about the same age as

her brother Mark stood grinning at her. He was wearing a dark gray suit and tie, a white shirt, and black dress shoes. Alison felt her cheeks redden as she snatched the veil off her head and dropped it on the bed. "Do I look like I'm ready to get married?" she asked.

"Are you the flower girl?" asked the boy.

"Of course not! I'm much too old for that." Even Alison knew that flower girls were usually really young. "I'm one of the bridesmaids." She gave him a haughty look.

"Sorry, I didn't realize that was an insult," he said.

Alison eyed the rug and smoothed her dress. Finally she sighed and looked him in the face. "That's okay. I . . . well, sometimes I fly off the handle. My name is Alison."

"Hi. I'm Adam, brother of the groom. I'm in the wedding, too." He had a slightly crooked smile and friendly brown eyes. "Look, I don't think I'm even supposed to be up here, but my mom sent me to give this to Jenny." He held out a small white box with a clear plastic lid.

"What is it?" Alison asked.

"Don't know." Adam shrugged. "Maybe you can figure it out. Here, read this." He handed the note from the box to Alison, and when she hesitated, he added, "Don't worry, Mom told me I could read it, so I guess it's okay for you, too."

Alison read it aloud: *My Dearest Jenny. My mother got this garter at a thrift shop in World War II. She wore it at her wedding and I wore it at mine. Here it is, as promised, for yours. I hope you'll be as happy with Ted as I've been with his father. Love, Harriet.* Alison turned the paper over, but there was nothing more written on it.

Adam handed her the box. "I've done my duty," he said, "and I'm going back outside. I made seven hook shots in a row before Mom sent me up here."

Alison's eyes lit up. "You have a basketball? Can I play? My record on hook shots is sixteen." She set the box and note on top of Jenny's dresser and turned back to Adam.

"You've got to be kidding."

"I am not. I play hoops a lot."

"Let's go," said Adam, and they raced down the stairs and out to the backyard. Adam picked up a basketball and bounce-passed it to Alison. She dribbled a few steps, then turned and arced a perfect hook into the basket.

"All riiight!" said Adam. "Okay, let's see if you can shoot against some defense." He grabbed at the ball, but Alison quickly put it on the ground and, keeping it low, dribbled around him for a layup. "Want to go one-on-one?"

Alison looked down at her dress and shoes. "I don't think I'd better. I might ruin my outfit. Knowing me, it's lucky I didn't already wreck it somehow."

"Oh, yeah," Adam said, pulling at his tie. "I hate wearing all this dress-up stuff. If I ever get married it's going to be in jeans and a T shirt."

"Or sweats," said Alison.

"Right," Adam replied, cracking a big grin. "Hey, the real reason I came out here was to find some junk to tie on the back of the getaway car. Want to help?"

"Sure," Alison replied. She hesitated for a moment, not sure whether to admit that she didn't know what he

was talking about. Oh, well, she thought, he's already seen me making a fool of myself in that veil. "What is a getaway car?" she asked shyly.

Adam glanced at her, then explained that after the ceremony and party, Ted and Jenny would drive away in Ted's red convertible and start their honeymoon. Adam had been assigned by the bridesmaids and the other ushers to attach the noisemakers to the bumper and decorate the car.

Alison followed Adam into the big, open garage. While he searched through the recycling barrels for noisy trash, she found a ball of twine on a shelf and began stringing cans and plastic bottles.

When they knelt to tie the cans to the car's rear bumper, Alison saw something white moving out of the corner of her eye. She turned to see what it was . . .

"Omigosh! It's the veil!" Alison shrieked. "Norton has Jenny's wedding veil!"

chapter Five

CRINOLINE
AND
ROSES

ithout a word, Alison and Adam shot out of the
garage, joining a throng of shouting
bridesmaids and ushers behind the speeding dog.
Suddenly Norton stopped and looked back at them,
giving the veil a little shake.

He wants us to chase him, thought Alison. He thinks this
is fun! She gathered her skirt in one hand and ran harder.

Norton skidded as he rounded a corner. He shot into
the big white tent where the food was being set up on

tables, then came flying out the back. His pursuers
scattered all around the yard, trying to head him off,
while Mrs. Morris and Jenny watched from the back porch
with horrified expressions.

Which way is he going to go now? Alison wondered. In
a split-second decision, she chose the left side of the
small stage and put on all the speed she could muster.
Suddenly, there he was, running straight at her! Alison
dove before he could turn around.

"You crazy dog!" she shouted, grabbing at the veil.

Then came a horrible ripping sound as Norton disappeared from sight, a big hunk of the veil trailing him. The rest was in Alison's hand.

Panting hard, Alison stood and pushed her flower headpiece out of her eyes. Then her breath caught in her throat. Mrs. Morris and Jenny were standing right in front of her. They seemed to be waiting for Alison to say something.

"I-I-I'm awfully sorry, Mrs. Morris. I thought he'd let go." Suddenly, Alison realized that she had more to tell. She looked around at the bridesmaids, who had gathered beside Mrs. Morris. Adam and the others had disappeared after Norton.

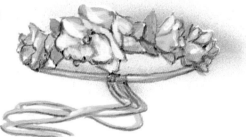

Alison took a big breath, then looked at Jenny and her mother and apologized for leaving the veil where Norton could get it. Alison held the tattered, dirty veil out for Jenny to see. "Norton has the other half," she added lamely, "and it's all my fault."

"That horrid dog!" Mrs. Morris said angrily. "Norton stays in the basement from now on." She took the veil and led the girls back to Jenny's room.

Jenny began to cry as her mother laid the ruined veil on the bed. Mrs. Morris and the bridesmaids were just getting her calmed down a little when Ted's mother walked in. "Are you nearly ready?" she asked cheerily, "Jenny, did Adam give you my garter? You know, I actually needed it to hold up my stocking when I—" She stopped in the middle of the sentence and stared at the remnant of the veil.

"There's not going to be any wedding," Jenny wailed.

Alison sat slumped on Jenny's chair, feeling more and more guilty. She knew it really wasn't her fault that Norton was such a rascal. But if she hadn't been trying on Jenny's wedding veil, this wouldn't have happened. Maybe she should just look into the mirror and go back home right now, before things got worse. Then her father's voice came back to her: "Alison, you're no quitter." He was right. There must be some way to fix things up, she thought, looking around the room.

Alison turned back to Jenny and the others. "Scarlett O'Hara!" she shouted.

"What?" asked Danielle, looking baffled.

"Scarlett O'Hara. You know, in *Gone with the Wind*."

"Alison," said Mrs. Morris, "I don't see what that has to do with—"

"The drapes!" Alison exclaimed. "Remember when Scarlett needed a new dress and didn't have any money to buy one? She made one from the green velvet drapes."

Everyone stared at Alison and then at Jenny's bright, yellow-flowered drapes. "I don't think they'd match her gown very well," Danielle replied sarcastically.

"No, I don't mean we should use the drapes. What I mean is, we have to find something we can use to make another veil."

"Oh, sure. No problem," Jenny said, flopping back on the bed. Her huge petticoat billowed up around her. "I just happen to have about a dozen wedding veils hidden in my running shoes!"

"Look, we still have the headband," Alison said. "If we wrap some new cloth around it, it'll be as good as new. We can decorate it with bits of lace or some flowers or something." Alison spun on her heel, looking quickly around the room. There must be something here that would work, she thought.

"I do have several pieces of satin," Jenny's mother offered.

Suddenly Alison froze and pointed at Jenny. "That's it!" she cried triumphantly.

"Look, Alison, just forget it, okay?" Jenny reached for the box of tissues again.

"Your petticoat!" shouted Alison. "That white net stuff, the crinoline or whatever it's called, is perfect for a veil."

"My crinoline petticoat?" Jenny cried, obviously horrified.

Mrs. Morris bent over the bed. "It's a little stiff," she

said, fingering the edge of Jenny's underskirt. "What do you think, Harriet?"

"There must be ten yards of crinoline here," said Ted's mother, "and we only need to take one panel out of it to make a veil. No one but us will ever know the difference."

"It'll never work," said Jenny, sniffling.

"Sure it will, Jenny," said Kelly.

"I'll go get my sewing box," said Mrs. Morris, hurrying from the room.

"And I'll find some flowers for it," said Alison, feeling the delicate crown of petals on her head. "I saw some just like mine outside the window."

"Alison, you be careful. And don't ruin your dress," Ted's mother admonished her.

"Yes, ma'am," said Alison, trying not to laugh. All mothers were alike, at least about some things. She had already played basketball, decorated a car, and chased the dog in it. She stepped out onto the balcony.

A rose-covered trellis ran up the back of the house. The prettiest blossoms were at the top of the latticework. Without giving it another thought, Alison leaned out until she was able to reach the prettiest of the roses. She carefully picked as big a bunch of fragrant pink blossoms as she could hold.

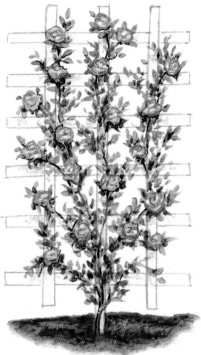

Then Alison looked down into the yard. Yikes, it must be really late, she thought. Most of the chairs were occupied, and a few guests were looking up at her and pointing.

"Need a ladder or a parachute or something?" a voice called up to her. It was Adam.

"Very funny!" Alison shouted. She made a comic little curtsy and darted back into the house. Jenny's mother had already covered the headband in shimmery white satin. She sat feverishly sewing a big swatch of crinoline to it as the bridesmaids restitched the seam of Jenny's underskirt as quickly as they could and Ted's mother arranged Jenny's curls. As she presented the pink flowers to Jenny, there was a knock at the door, and a man's voice called, "Jenny, I need to talk to you for a minute."

"Ted!" Jenny shrieked. "Don't you dare come in here!"

Ted's mother waved at Kelly. "Send him away. He knows he can't see his bride on the day of the wedding until she meets him at the altar. It's bad luck."

Kelly hurried over and talked quietly to Ted through the closed door.

When the veil and petticoat were finished, Mrs. Morris looked at her watch and exclaimed, "Jennifer, get dressed. The ceremony is supposed to start in ten minutes."

"Come on, Jenny, hop into your gown," Whitney said. "It's also bad luck for the bride to appear at the altar in her underwear!" The room was a flurry of activity as all the bridesmaids helped Jenny into her long, lacy white gown. They carefully placed the veil on her head as she slipped her feet into a pair of elegant satin slippers.

Chapter
Six

A FITTING TOAST

ith a last glance in the mirror, everyone hurried downstairs. The ushers escorted Jenny's mother and Ted's mother to their seats, and as the bridesmaids gathered at the big French doors that opened onto the back lawn, the string quartet began to play the processional music. The guests oohed and aahed when the little ring bearer and flower girl appeared in the doorway.

Alison peeked out into the yard. She took a sharp breath. The white runner that formed the aisle seemed to stretch ahead for miles. She knew bridesmaids were supposed to walk down the aisle in some slow, special way, but she had no idea how. Mark was always telling her she walked like a linebacker.

The flower girl was tossing rose petals from her basket, with the ring bearer following solemnly behind her. They were nearly a quarter of the way down the aisle already, but Alison stood rooted to the spot.

"You lead, Alison," said Danielle. "Go ahead, you'll do fine. Everyone's waiting to see the bride."

She had to move! Alison stepped onto the white runner and moved forward, one hesitant step at a time, copying the four-year-old ring bearer's walk.

When all the bridesmaids had taken their place at the altar, the guests rose from their seats to watch Jenny and her father make their slow walk across the lawn. She really does look pretty, Alison thought. It seemed like a dream as Jenny and Ted exchanged their vows and he took the ring and slipped it onto her finger. Then they kissed and walked back down the aisle together. When they left through the

French doors, everyone stood up and walked across the lawn for the reception.

Dozens of white wicker tables were set with flowered place mats, pink napkins, and gleaming silverware. Inside the enormous white tent, tables were piled high with all sorts of food.

A waiter appeared with a trayful of glasses and stopped right in front of Alison. "Can I take two?" she whispered, and the waiter nodded. She took a couple of glasses of fruit punch and drank them.

"Come with me," said Danielle, pointing to the polished wooden dance floor that had been set up right over the lawn. She led Alison to the large table on the right side of the stage. On it was a spectacular four-tiered wedding cake frosted in white with pink flowers and garlands. The bride and groom figures on the top were framed by a delicate heart-shaped ornament. Guests began tapping their glasses with the silverware, and Jenny and Ted stepped onto the stage.

One of the ushers, a sandy-haired young man named Jack, stepped up to the bandstand microphone.

"Oh, there's the best man," said a woman standing behind Alison and Danielle.

"I want to offer the first toast to the new bride and groom," Jack said, and everyone quieted down. After congratulating Ted and Jenny, he told some jokes about people Alison had never heard of, and her mind wandered. Hearing Norton's name got her attention, though. ". . . probably all saw him tearing around the yard with Jenny's veil, and saw us chasing after him like a bunch of Keystone Cops." Some people laughed, but Alison wanted to crawl under the bandstand even though Danielle gave her arm an affectionate squeeze.

"Well," Jack continued, "that just shows that all kinds of things can go wrong anytime. I'd like to raise a toast to our Jenny, who had the good sense and the 'smarts' to fix everything and go ahead with the really important stuff— like marrying my best friend, Ted."

"Hear! Hear!" shouted several guests, and everyone applauded again. Jack raised his glass to the newlyweds, but he didn't drink until Jenny and Ted sipped from each other's glasses.

The dance band began to play. Alison knew she had heard the tune before, but she couldn't remember where or what it was called. She watched as Mr. Morris took Jenny's hand and led her to the middle of the floor. She

thought Jenny's eyes looked tearful as she twirled around with her father. Then the band eased right into a new tune, and the other family members started dancing. Mr. Morris handed Jenny over to Ted and led Ted's mother to dance, while Mrs. Morris waltzed with Ted's father. Then they switched around again, so that each of them was with his or her own husband or wife.

After that, Alison lost track of who was whose partner. She went to a quiet spot and relaxed until she heard Mrs. Morris's voice on the microphone, calling the bridesmaids and ushers to the front of the stage. When Alison had worked her way up beside the others, Jenny and Ted were holding a cake knife and cutting off big, gooey slices of the wedding cake while a photographer snapped picture after picture. They twined their arms together like some strange pretzel and managed to each hold a piece of cake. Ted laughed as he took a bite from his piece while Jenny ate from hers, and they ended up with frosting all over their chins and hands. Everyone laughed and cheered as the couple toasted the crowd with their slices of wedding cake.

Chapter Seven

YOU'RE
NEXT,
ALISON!

enny wiped her hands, cut generous wedges of
cake, and handed one to each member of the
wedding party. As she leaned over to give a plateful to
Alison, she whispered, "Alison, I'm sorry I got so upset
earlier. I was pretty nervous. Jack's toast really should
have been to you—you're the one who figured out how to
patch everything up." She leaned even closer. "You know,
when I was your age, I was a lot like you. I'm glad you
were part of my big day, and I hope you are, too."

"Thanks a lot, Jenny," said Alison, sneaking a little frosting onto her finger and licking it off. She wandered back to one of the tables near the stage, sat down, and watched the dancing while she ate. She didn't really know anyone, so there was no one to talk to.

Then a familiar voice mumbled, "Mind if I sit here, too?"

It was Adam. "Okay," said Alison. She didn't want him to know how happy she was to have someone join her. She glanced at his plate. "Oh, are you just now getting your cake?"

Adam laughed. "Are you kidding? This is my third."

"Your third? Adam!" It was his mother. "If you're on your third slice of cake, then you haven't danced yet. You and Alison get out there on that dance floor and have some fun."

"Mom, we *are* having fun," said Adam.

Mrs. Morris came up behind Alison and gently moved her plate to the center of the table. "Go ahead, both of you," she said, laughing. "We'll sit right here and make sure no one takes your cake away while you're dancing."

Alison felt her cheeks turning red.

Adam's mother sat down. She gave Adam a look and pulled his plate away, too.

Alison and Adam looked at each other. Adam sighed, then stood up and asked, "Well, do you want to dance?" He didn't sound too thrilled.

"Adam, mind your manners," said his mother.

"Alison, would you care to share this dance with me?" Adam asked sullenly, holding out his hand.

Alison couldn't help but laugh as she got up and followed him onto the dance floor. The band was playing a slow song.

"I hate all this mushy romantic stuff," Adam said, shaking his head and grimacing.

"I'm not very good at this, either," replied Alison. "Anyhow, they'll probably let us off the hook pretty soon." They stood swaying in one spot. Alison tried to think of something to say. Then she remembered the getaway car.

"Hey," she said, "didn't we forget something? I didn't see 'Just Married' on the car anywhere."

"I completely forgot!" Adam thought for a moment. "I saw some shaving cream in the downstairs bathroom. We can use that to write with. Come on!"

They ran off to finish the job on Ted's car. They took turns lettering JUST MARRIED on the hood,

trunk, and both sides, laughing as they handed the can
back and forth.

"Think they'd get really mad if we sprayed the seats?"
asked Adam.

Alison nodded. "Yes, I think they'd get really mad. . . .
Wait a minute, though." She sprayed a big, open heart on
the passenger side of the windshield, with an arrow right
through the center. With a flourish, she bowed and
handed the shaving cream to Adam. He made a large,
sloppy heart on the driver's side.

"Cool," said Alison.

"Yeah," Adam said. "Slap me five."

They slapped hands and headed back to their table.
Mrs. Morris and Adam's mother were gone and so was
the cake. "Well, now there's nothing to do," said Adam.
"The music's a little better than before, though. I listen to
this song a lot." He looked around as if he was making
sure no one was close enough to hear. "Want to try it
again?" he asked, nodding toward the dance floor.

"I guess," said Alison. Adam's dancing wasn't bad
at all this time, and Alison certainly felt more
comfortable than before, bopping around in time with
the beat. Then the bandleader announced that it was
time for the bride to toss her bouquet. Kelly ran up
and grabbed Alison's arm. "Come on or we'll miss it,"

she said, pulling Alison toward the house.

"Miss what?" Alison asked. "What's happening?"

"We have to try to catch Jenny's bouquet when she throws it," Kelly answered.

All the guests had gathered again, this time below Jenny's balcony, with the bridesmaids at the front of the crowd. Kelly pushed through to join Whitney and Danielle, saying softly, "Excuse us, excuse us please," again and again.

"Oh, we missed Jenny's little good-bye speech." Kelly sounded very disappointed.

"At least you're in time for the bouquet, though," said Danielle, patting Kelly on the shoulder.

Alison looked up. Ted was standing in the doorway and Jenny was at the balcony railing with her back to the guests. She raised the flowers in front of her face with both hands, then tossed them back over her head. The bouquet went sailing, and for Alison it was an easy catch. All she had to do was jump up and reach out, and there were the pink and white flowers in her hand. The guests gave a round of applause as Jenny walked over to Ted and they disappeared into the house.

"Well, Alison," said Danielle with a smile, "I guess you're the next to be married!"

"What!" cried Alison.

Kelly laughed. "Oh, Alison, didn't you know? Whoever catches the bride's wedding bouquet is supposed to be the next one to get married."

Alison nearly dropped the bouquet.

"Come on, let's see them off," shouted Whitney. "Get your rice and birdseed ready." The bridesmaids and ushers hurried toward the driveway.

I think that's my cue to exit, thought Alison. She sprinted up the stairs to Jenny's room and took a last look around. The wedding gown and petticoat were neatly hung over the closet door, and the puffy crinoline veil was draped over a chair. Alison ran her fingers over the veil, then went onto the balcony. Ted and Jenny were just pulling out of the driveway. The low-slung red car looked great with all the gooey white lettering, and the junk that Alison and Adam had attached made lots of noise as the car disappeared down the street.

Alison closed the door and carefully picked up the veil. She couldn't resist trying it on again just for a moment. One day she might wear one like it in her own wedding. She would have Keisha, Megan, and Heather as her bridesmaids. . . . She put the veil back and walked over to Jenny's mirror.

As Alison looked at herself once more in the beautiful blue dress, her reflection seemed to quiver a little, and

she held the bouquet tightly. She thought she heard
Norton. But when she looked for the cocker spaniel, she
was back in the wonderful
attic, and she realized it
was Ellie's dog, Monty,
that was barking.

chapter Eight

ALISON SAVES THE DAY

Alison set the key back in its silver box in Ellie's hallway. The sounds of a violin came from the room where Ellie gave music lessons, so Alison knew that the soprano had left and another student had arrived. She stepped quietly to the door and let herself out. She would just make it home in time to help with dinner.

After dinner, Alison telephoned her friends to call a meeting of the Magic Attic Club for early the next morning at Heather's house. "It's too late now to tell you what happened in Ellie's attic," she told Heather. "But I have this great idea for our precision bike-riding team."

"Does this involve jumping off a building or something?" asked Heather.

Alison laughed. "No. I'll tell you all about it tomorrow."

The next morning the other members of the Magic Attic Club were already in the Hardins' kitchen when Alison arrived. The girls decided that even though they all had eaten at home, a piece of Mr. Hardin's raisin bread French toast with powdered sugar would hit the spot. Alison excitedly raced through her tale of the wedding while they ate their second breakfast.

"Ali, only you would think of playing basketball in a bridesmaid's outfit!" said Megan.

Alison grinned. "It wasn't a good idea. It's really hard to dribble in a long dress."

"McCann," said Keisha, "you are a complete and total sports maniac. I can hardly imagine you in a full-length dress. And with flowers in your hair, yet!"

"I wish I could have been there," Heather said with a sigh. "I would love to be in a real wedding."

Suddenly Alison jumped up with a gleam in her eye.

"Heather, bring your colored pencils outside. There's something you have to sketch for me."

"Let me guess," said Keisha. "A wedding gown with a team logo on it."

"Oh, come on, you guys," said Alison. Then she was out the door.

Heather lifted her hands, palms up, and gave Keisha and Megan an I-don't-know look as she went to get her art supplies. The girls hurried outside and found Alison standing on her hands beside her beat-up bicycle in the driveway.

"So what do you want me to sketch?" asked Heather.

"This is it," said Alison, pointing to her bike as she lowered her feet to the ground.

"You must be kidding," said Keisha. "You can't want a picture to remind you of *that* for the rest of your life, can you?"

"Exactly the opposite," Alison replied. "I want to turn this mess into something fantastic, just like we did with Jenny's veil."

"I get it," Heather said. "If we paint the bike just right, it'll look even better than it did before the accident."

"Cool!" shouted Megan and Keisha.

"But I think we need some special kind of paint," Heather continued. "Let's ask my mom."

The four of them found Mrs. Hardin working upstairs

in her art studio and insisted that she go
out to look at the bike. "Oh, Alison," she
said when she saw it, "you
really did a job on this
poor thing!"

"I sure did," said
Alison. She turned to the
girls. "I thought it was all
fixed after you left. When I test-rode it last night, though,
it was awfully wobbly. Mark and I worked on it for a whole
hour, and it works great now. We had to take the fenders
off and hammer the dents out. It looks awful, but all it
really needs is a new coat of paint. I was hoping you and
Heather could help me come up with something neat to
do with it."

Mrs. Hardin put her arm around her daughter and
Alison. "How about if all five of us put our heads
together? Bring the bike into the studio and we'll see
what we can do."

Alison wheeled the bike inside and lugged it upstairs.
Mrs. Hardin brought out a color chart of a special, shiny
enamel that was made for painting metal, and they all
tried various color combinations on a sketch of the bike
to see what might work.

Alison, of course, got to make the final decision.

She chose a base of her favorite color, robin's-egg blue. She'd paint a golden ribbon all up and down the entire frame and fenders. She wanted a garland of red, white, and blue bunting to drape over the handlebars, with matching crepe paper streamers strung through the spokes. The design was complete.

"It's going to be fabulous," said Megan. "I want to do my bike, too. This is so much better than that awful pink and purple design it came with."

"What's wrong with pink?" asked Heather, pretending to be terribly insulted.

"Or purple, *my* favorite color?" Keisha added.

"You've seen my bike," Megan replied. "It's stomach-medicine pink and grape-soda purple."

"Yuck!" said Mrs. Hardin, and everyone laughed.

All the girls wanted to paint their bikes and their parade outfits, and Mrs. Hardin agreed to help if they got permission from their parents.

The four friends spent the next two days practicing their routine and working with Mrs. Hardin in her studio. Heather had chosen shocking pink for her base color; Megan had gone with her favorite, yellow; and of course Keisha couldn't live without purple. They each got a T shirt in their own color, then painted their bikes the same shade. Heather and her mother sketched the

designs onto the bikes and the clothing, and each girl did the painstaking work of painting in the details on her own bike, T shirt, and shoes with tiny, pointed paintbrushes.

Chapter

Nine

HAPPY
FOURTH!

lison was up at daybreak on the Fourth of July, shining every inch of her bike and practicing her routine in the empty dead-end street. She thought it would never be time to leave for the parade.

When she finally arrived at the main square downtown, an enormous crowd was milling around. It was a good thing that she and the girls had decided exactly where they'd meet. They were surrounded by marching bands, groups of riders on horseback, antique cars, floats made by local organizations, and even little kids leading their costumed pets. Finally, one of the parade marshals directed them into line between a group of tumbling clowns and a high school band.

"A whole flock of butterflies just landed in my stomach," cried Megan.

"Relax," said Heather. "With all these acts, nobody's even going to notice us." She sounded disappointed.

Keisha nodded. "Right," she said, her voice glum. "We might as well be the invisible bike-riding team."

Alison tried to find something to cheer them up. "What do you want to bet we're the only precision bike-riding team in the parade?"

"So?" asked Keisha.

"So, we don't really have any competition," said Alison triumphantly. Megan managed a weak smile, but Keisha and Heather rolled their eyes.

Then the parade marshal blew her whistle, and all the bands began to play. The parade was underway!

The clowns in front of the girls flipped and somersaulted down the street, spraying the crowd with water and confetti, and the girls couldn't

help but laugh. The four of them mounted up, and as they turned the corner onto the main parade route, they began their routine. They knew every move by heart, and the enormous sound of the bands gave them a precise rhythm they had never had before.

"This is the best we've ever done it, you guys!" Alison shouted over the din. "Keep it up!"

As the team neared the judges' stand, Alison saw her parents and brothers on the side of the street. Her three best friends' families stood clapping right alongside them. Ellie was sandwiched between Mark and Jenna, Heather's older sister.

Exercising her authority as captain, Alison called for one of their most difficult and showy moves, the one the girls had secretly named the Magic Attic Spin. They wheeled into it and performed it perfectly. Everyone cheered wildly, and Mark flashed a thumbs-up. Cameras clicked away as the girls waved and pedaled toward the reviewing stand.

The clowns had done their silliest stuff, and the judges were still laughing as the girls rode to a smart stop in front of the stand. Great, thought Alison, they're in a good mood.

She raised her right hand to call the team to attention, then snapped a military salute to the judges.

The moment she dropped her salute, the team wheeled into their routine. They bobbed and weaved as they made intersecting figure eights, then moved smoothly into a short series of precision turns. The bright, stiff cards on their rear wheels clicked against the spokes as they executed perfect wheelies back toward the judges. Then they fanned out to an abrupt stop a few feet from the stand, stood up on the bike seats, and gave a quick bow.

The moment Alison saw one of the bikes begin to wobble, she gave the dismount signal. The cheers and applause seemed to double when the judges saluted the team. With huge smiles, the girls pedaled away to finish out the parade route.

Their families had staked out two picnic tables in the park and put them together, and Ellie was turning hot dogs on the grill when the girls rode up. All four were tired from the heat and exertion, but they couldn't seem to wipe the grins from their faces.

"You were great, Ali," said Mark. He handed plastic glasses of iced tea to his sister and her friends.

"Thanks, Mark." Alison quickly dained her glass and

got herself a refill.

"You sure were," said Mr. McCann, patting his daughter on the back.

Alison gave her father a big smile. "I just hope we win something," she added.

"Win or lose," said Mrs. McCann, "I'm awfully proud of you for coming up with such a great idea."

"I am, too," said Ellie, coming over to hug the girls.

"Well, I really got it from the Chinese," said Alison.

"What did you say?" asked her father. He and Mrs. McCann stared at Alison.

"The Chinese," she repeated. "And a wedding veil— and Ellie, too."

"Alison," said her father, "sometimes I don't have the faintest notion what you're talking about."

Alison winked at Ellie. Then Heather, Megan, and Keisha gathered around her, and they high-fived in unison.

Diary

Dear Diary,

This has been the most fantastic Fourth of July ever. Our bike team won a special trophy in the parade for having "The Most Imaginative Vehicles," and our pictures will be in the Herald tomorrow. We're practically famous! Mark wants his bike painted with rockets and planets and other space stuff. Of course I reminded him that I was the one who thought of this whole neat idea.

While we were standing on the judges' platform getting our trophy, I was thinking that none of this would have happened if my bike hadn't been squashed under the car. It's funny how a problem that seems so awful at the time can actually work out to be a good thing.

Oh, gosh, I almost forgot to tell you. I was a

bridesmaid in a wedding. Can you imagine <u>me</u> as a bridesmaid? Just between us, that blue dress and the crown of roses weren't so bad.

That started out to be a disaster, too. But I remembered what Ellie had said to me about opportunity, and I actually ended up saving Jenny's wedding!

Lately it's almost like there's no such thing as bad luck. I hope I can remember that the next time something goes wrong.

Well, I have to close, it's bedtime.

Love, Me

Alison